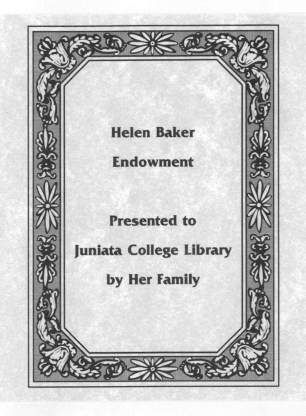

Silver Threads

Silver Threads

Marsha Forchuk Skrypuch

Illustrations by Michael Martchenko

Fitzhenry & Whiteside

This project has been funded in part by the Ukrainian Canadian Foundation of Taras Shevchenko.

Published in Canada by
Fitzhenry & Whiteside,
195 Allstate Parkway,
Markham, Ontario
L3R 4T8

Published in the United States by
Fitzhenry & Whiteside,
121 Harvard Avenue, Suite 2,
Allston, Massachusetts
02134

www.fitzhenry.ca   godwit@fitzhenry.ca

10 9 8 7 6 5 4 3 2 1

National Library of Canada Cataloguing in Publication

Skrypuch, Marsha Forchuk, 1954-
Silver threads / by Marsha Forchuk Skrypuch ; illustrated by Michael Martchenko.

Originally published in Canada by Viking, Toronto, 1996.
ISBN 1-55041-901-3 (bound). ISBN 1-55041-903-X (pbk.)

1. World War, 1914-1918–Ukrainian Canadians–Juvenile fiction.
2. World War, 1914-1918–Concentration camps–Canada–Juvenile fiction.
3. World War, 1914-1918–Evacuation of civilians–Canada–Juvenile fiction.
4. Ukrainian Canadians–Juvenile fiction. I. Martchenko, Michael II. Title.

PS8587.K79S5 2004   jC813'.54   C2004-900830-7

Publisher Cataloging-in-Publication Data (U.S.)
(Library of Congress Standard)

Skrypuch, Marsha Forchuk.

Silver threads / by Marsha Forchuk Skrypuch ; illustrated by Michael Martchenko.
Originally published: Penguin Books Canada, 1996.
[32] p. : col. ill. ; cm.
Summary: Anna and Ivan, two young newlyweds, escape poverty and hardship in Ukraine to start a new life on the
Canadian Frontier. As they struggle to establish themselves, World War I breaks out, and Ivan is taken prisoner as an enemy.
ISBN 1-55041-901-3
ISBN 1-55041-903-X (pbk.)
1. Canada–History–1914-1945 – Juvenile fiction.
(1. Canada – History –1914-1945 – Fiction.)   I. Martchenko, Michael, ill. II. Title.
[E] 22   PZ7.S577Si 1996

Fitzhenry & Whiteside acknowledges with thanks the Canada Council for the Arts, the Government of Canada
through the Book Publishing Industry Development Program (BPIDP), and the Ontario Arts Council
for their support of our publishing program.

Design by Wycliffe Smith

Printed in Hong Kong

In memory of George and Anna Forchuk, whose experiences inspired this book

M.S.

_____

To my mother, whose love and devotion gave me the opportunity to achieve my ambition in a new land.
Thank you, Ma

M.M.

Silver Threads was made possible with the help of the following friends:
Gail Winskill, Doreen Potter, Martina Boone,
Professor Lubomyr Luciuk and Marusia Petryshyn.

In a land called Bukovyna, in Ukraine, a husband and wife farmed their narrow strip of land.

"It takes two of us," Ivan would say. "One to push the plough and one to pull."

One afternoon, Ivan stopped. "What's that sound?"

"Shouts," said Anna. "From the village."

They raced to a hill that overlooked the Village Square. Hidden behind a tree, Anna and Ivan watched in horror as soldiers chained the village men and marched them away.

Anna and Ivan ran home.

The old woman that lived next door hobbled towards them. "Put this on," she told Ivan. "The soldiers will soon be back." She threw a babushka, a shawl, over his shoulders.

"What does the foreign emperor want now?" Ivan asked.

"He needs more soldiers to help him steal other lands as he has stolen ours," she explained.

Ivan pushed the babushka away. "I will not fight for this emperor, but I am not a coward who hides from soldiers."

"But what else can we do?" Anna asked.

"There is another way," said the woman. "A sign was posted in the village last month. It told of a country called 'Canada' across the ocean. It is a land of milk and honey, with plenty of black soil but not enough farmers to plough it. One hundred and sixty acres are waiting for anyone brave enough to claim them."

One hundred and sixty acres? It seemed impossible! After all, Ivan and Anna's farm was a mere two acres.

That night, Ivan removed the one pane of glass from the window and wrapped it in the babushka. Anna took the hinges from the door. Then Ivan walked to the corner of the house where a black spider had spun a long silvery thread and woven it into a beautiful web. "Little spider, this will be the last time I feed you," he said, "but now we will need your good luck more than ever."

He sprinkled breadcrumbs in front of the web, and in the darkness Anna and Ivan left their home.

With tears in their eyes, Anna and Ivan stepped onto the ship. They travelled across the ocean to Canada. The ship overflowed with people. As it tossed about on the waves, the two found refuge on a slat of wood in a dark corner. There a spider slowly spun out its web, unaware of the rollicking sea.

When the ship landed, Ivan and Anna found their journey was far from over. This part of Canada had no land to spare for newcomers. With the others from the ship, they travelled by train for days over the vast, flat country.

The new soil was indeed as black and rich as the sign had promised. But the sign hadn't said that the land was covered with trees. And that the winters were so cold, a flask of water could freeze before it reached the lips.

But Anna and Ivan were happy.

They built a one-room home amid the wilderness. The pane of glass served as their one window. The hinges opened and closed their new door. And a tiny black spider nestled in a corner, spinning its threads of silver. Though food was scarce, Ivan always found a few crumbs to sprinkle in front of the web.

The thousands of trees that covered their land had to be removed one by one. It was backbreaking work, but Anna and Ivan didn't mind. After all, there were two of them—one to push the saw and one to pull. By spring Ivan and Anna had sawed down three acres of trees. They traded the wood for sacks of food.

Next, Ivan and Anna began removing the tree stumps. By planting time, a single acre had been cleared. They planted their first small crop of wheat.

Though they were miles from the nearest village, their door was always open to those who travelled across the country to claim farms of their own. One day they heard that Canada too had gone to war against the foreign emperor.

"I could not save Bukovyna," declared Ivan, "but Canada is my country now. And I must fight."

Their last night together was Sviat Vecher—Christmas Eve. With a heavy heart, Anna prepared the meatless dishes, then counted to make sure she had the traditional twelve.

She set a sheaf of wheat—a didukh—in the corner of the room. Then she and Ivan cut down a firtree. It was not a difficult job for two—one to push the saw and the other to pull.

Ivan decorated the tree with cookies and a few shiny apples. But the festive house made them feel even sadder. Early Christmas morning they walked hand in hand to the distant village so that Ivan could enlist as a soldier.

"It will be hard for you to run the homestead by yourself," he told Anna. "You can push, but I won't be there to pull."

"I'll manage somehow," she said, squeezing his hand.

They approached the town hall, passing a group of prisoners in chains. "Don't go in there," one of the prisoners called to them in their own language. But Anna and Ivan ignored him.

The official glared at Ivan. "What do you want?"

"I want to fight for Canada," said Ivan. "For my country."

"You don't sound like a Canadian."

"I was born in Bukovyna," said Ivan, "but my country is Canada."

"Bukovyna is part of the Emperor's land. You are an enemy of Canada."

"The Emperor stole Bukovyna from Ukraine!" Anna cried.

The official didn't listen. He shackled Ivan's wrists and dragged him to where the other prisoners were chained.

"Go home!" Ivan called to Anna. "Protect our homestead. We'll share another Sviat Vecher, I promise."

Anna cried herself to sleep that night, wrapped in the babushka for warmth. The house was so silent. So still.

When Anna opened her eyes the next day, light was shining through the pane of glass. In the corner of the window, sparkling in the light, was a silver web made by Ivan's spider.

Just as Ivan had done, Anna made sure the spider always had a few crumbs in front of its web.

Without Ivan to help, she couldn't cut down any more trees or remove any more stumps. But Anna planted wheat in the acre of cleared soil and planted vegetables around the stumps. Years passed with no word from her husband. Her store of food got smaller.

As each Sviat Vecher came and went, Anna found herself alone.

She refused to give up hope, remembering Ivan's last words, "We'll share another Sviat Vecher, I promise."

One year, before the first snowflakes of winter fell to the ground, there was a knock on Anna's door.

"You'll have to give up your homestead," the official said, eyeing the farm with a gleam in his eye. "Your agreement says that you must clear some land each year, and you haven't done that."

"But you took my husband away and I cannot clear it myself."

"Don't you know the war has ended?" he asked. "If your husband isn't home by now, he must be dead."

This was too much for Anna. She slumped on the doorstep and cradled her head in her hands.

The man's expression softened. "I suppose I could give you until next spring."

Anna worked busily that autumn, bringing in her scanty harvest. As Christmas approached, she still had not heard from Ivan. "I know in my heart that he is alive," she told the spider.

She swept the house thoroughly, making sure not to disturb the spider's web. Then she washed the walls and laundered the babushka and spread it on the scrubbed table. She looked at her thin store of food.

"Hmmm" Anna said. "It will take imagination to make the traditional twelve dishes from this."

But she set to work, making a spoonful of the grain pudding known as kutia, two pyrohy, and two holubtsi—cabbage rolls. She had one beet, so she made a cup of borscht. With her last bit of flour she made a tiny braided kolach. "Each mouthful will have to count as a dish," she mused.

Anna searched the field for what scattered stalks of wheat were left, and bound them into a tiny didukh. She placed it in the corner. And then she set the table for two. Alone, she cut a firtree and dragged it back to the house. It was hard work for one person. She could push the saw, but Ivan wasn't there to pull.

She set a candle before the pane of glass, hoping that its light might guide Ivan home.

As the first star appeared, Anna prayed for her husband's return.

But Ivan did not come. The candle sputtered and died. Shivering, Anna pulled the babushka from the table and wrapped herself in it, then cried herself to sleep.

The sun shining through the window warmed her cheek. Her heart was so full of despair that she was afraid to open her eyes. She thought of the cold food, the bare tree and the empty house. With a sigh, she rose.

She drew a breath in wonder. The forlorn tree had been transformed, dazzling in a tapestry of silvery threads. On the topmost branch, the black spider slept, resting from an evening of labour.

The hinges of the door creaked. Anna turned and …

... there stood Ivan—tired, but alive.

Anna ran to the door and wrapped her arms around her husband. "You've come home."

"I promised you I would," said Ivan.

"But the war ended months ago!" cried Anna.

"I escaped from the internment camp," he said, "and hid in the woods. I just heard that the war has ended." He gazed at the silvered firtree. "This is what I saw through the window. If it weren't for those silver threads, I might still be searching for home."

So Anna and Ivan had a joyous Sviat Vecher, even if the food was cold and a day late.

Now that there were two of them, they cleared the rest of the stumps in the first spring thaw. When the official returned, he was amazed at their progress.

"She pushes and I pull," Ivan explained, his hand firmly clasped in Anna's.

HISTORICAL NOTE

During World War I, twenty-four internment camps were set up across the country. Thousands of innocent Ukrainians and other Europeans were imprisoned as "enemy aliens." These were men, women and children who had done no wrong but were hated because of where they had come from. They were forced to do heavy labour, and their personal belongings were taken. The government did not shut down the internment operations until two years after the end of World War I.

To this day, the government has not acknowledged this injustice, nor have they returned the confiscated belongings.

My grandfather, George Forchuk, was interned at Jasper in 1914.

Resources

Online:
Teacher's guide to Silver Threads:
http://calla.com/silverguide.html
Ukrainian internment during WWI:
http://www.infoukes.com/history/internment/

Book:
Luciuk, Lubomyr Y.; Sorobey,
Ron; Carynnyk, Marco (translator);
Carynnyk, Marta (translator). In Fear of the Barbed
Wire Fence: Canada's first National Internment Operations
and the Ukrainian Canadians, 1914-1920. Kingston, Kashtan Press, 2001.

film:
Luhovy, Yurij, director/producer. Freedom Had a Price. Ottawa, National Film Board of Canada, 1994.